MAG

Magee, Wes,
   1939-

Row, row, row your
boat.

$22.60   Preschool    10/18/2013

| DATE | | |
|---|---|---|
| | | |
| | | |
| | | |
| | | |
| | | |
| | | |
| | | |
| | | |
| | | |
| | | |
| | | |
| | | |

# Row, Row, Row Your Boat

and

# Ride, Ride, Ride Your Bike

**Retold by Wes Magee**

**Illustrated by Marina Le Ray**

**Crabtree Publishing Company**

www.crabtreebooks.com

 **Crabtree Publishing Company**
www.crabtreebooks.com
1-800-387-7650

PMB 59051, 350 Fifth Ave.
59th Floor,
New York, NY 10118

616 Welland Ave.
St. Catharines, ON
L2M 5V6

Published by Crabtree Publishing in 2013
Printed in Hong Kong/012013/BK20121102

Series editor: Melanie Palmer
Editor: Kathy Middleton
Notes for adults: Reagan Miller
Series advisors: Dr. Hilary Minns, Catherine Glavina
Series designer: Peter Scoulding
Production coordinator and
   Prepress technician: Margaret Amy Salter
Print coordinator: Katherine Berti

Text (Ride, Ride, Ride Your Bike)
© Wes Magee 2010
Illustration © Marina Le Ray 2010

The rights of Wes Magee to be
identified as the author of Ride,
Ride, Ride Your Bike and Marina
Le Ray as the illustrator of
this Work have been asserted.

First published in 2010
by Franklin Watts
(A division of Hachette
Children's Books)

**Library and Archives Canada
Cataloguing in Publication**

Magee, Wes, 1939-
    Row, row, row your boat ; and, Ride, ride,
ride your bike / retold by Wes Magee ; illustrated
by Marina Le Ray.

(Tadpoles: nursery rhymes)
Issued also in electronic format.
ISBN 978-0-7787-1149-0 (bound).--ISBN 978-0-
7787-1153-7 (pbk.)

    1. Nursery rhymes, English. I. Le Ray,
Marina II. Title. III. Title: Ride, ride, ride your
bike. IV. Series: Tadpoles (St. Catharines, Ont.).
Nursery rhymes

PZ8.3.M34Ro 2013     j398.8     C2012-907344-X

**Library of Congress
Cataloging-in-Publication Data**

Magee, Wes, 1939-
[Poetry. Selections]
Row, row, row your boat ; and Ride, ride, your
bike / retold by Wes Magee ; illustrated by Marina Le
Ray.
    pages cm. -- (Tadpoles: nursery rhymes)
    Summary: Presents the traditional nursery rhyme, a
line at a time then as a whole, followed by a new
rhyme. Includes "Notes for adults" and reading tips.
    ISBN 978-0-7787-1149-0 (reinforced library binding :
alk. paper) -- ISBN 978-0-7787-1153-7 (pbk. : alk.
paper) -- ISBN 978-1-4271-9309-4 (electronic pdf) --
ISBN 978-1-4271-9233-2 (electronic html)
    1. Nursery rhymes. 2. Children's poetry. [1. Nursery
rhymes.] I. Le Ray, Marina, illustrator. II. Magee,
Wes, 1939- Row, row, row your boat III. Magee, Wes,
1939- Ride, ride, ride your bike IV. Title.

    PZ8.3.M2685Ro 2013
    398.8--dc23

                                        2012043747

# Row, Row, Row Your Boat

**Marina
Le Ray**

"I like the idea of rowing a boat down a stream on a lovely, sunny day, and all the wildlife you would see along the way."

# Row, row, row
## your boat

gently down
the stream.

# Merrily, merrily,

merrily, merrily,

# life is but a dream.

# Row, Row, Row
# Your Boat

Row, row, row your boat
gently down the stream.
Merrily, merrily,
merrily, merrily,
life is but a dream.

Can you point to the
rhyming words?

# Ride, Ride, Ride Your Bike

**Wes Magee**

"The first time
I tried to ride
my new bike, I went
too fast down the
lane, and I fell off!"

# Ride, ride, ride your bike

up the muddy lane.

Bumpity, bumpity,
bumpity, bumpity,

ride it back again.

# Puzzle Time!

**1.**

**2.**

**3.**

Choose the right action
for the picture.

# Notes for adults

**TADPOLES NURSERY RHYMES** are structured for emergent readers. The books may also be used for read-alouds or shared reading with young children.

The language of nursery rhymes is often already familiar to an emergent reader. Seeing the rhymes in print helps build phonemic awareness skills. The alternative rhymes extend and enhance the reading experience further, and encourage children to be creative with language and make up their own rhymes.

## IF YOU ARE READING THIS BOOK WITH A CHILD, HERE ARE A FEW SUGGESTIONS:

1. Make reading fun! Choose a time to read when you and the child are relaxed and have time to share the story.

2. Recite the nursery rhyme together before you start reading. What might the alternative rhyme be about? Brainstorm ideas.

3. Encourage the child to reread the rhyme and to retell it using his or her own words. Invite the child to use the illustrations as a guide.

4. Help the child identify the rhyming words when the whole rhymes are repeated on pages 12 and 22. This activity builds phonological awareness and decoding skills. Encourage the child to make up alternative rhymes.

5. Give praise! Children learn best in a positive environment.

## IF YOU ENJOYED THIS BOOK, WHY NOT TRY ANOTHER TITLE FROM TADPOLES: NURSERY RHYMES?

**VISIT WWW.CRABTREEBOOKS.COM FOR OTHER CRABTREE BOOKS.**

# Answer

The correct action is picture 3.

24

# Ride, Ride, Ride Your Bike

Ride, ride, ride your bike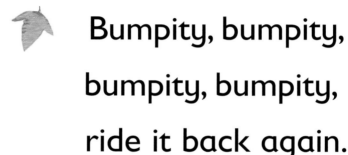

up the muddy lane.

Bumpity, bumpity,

bumpity, bumpity,

ride it back again.

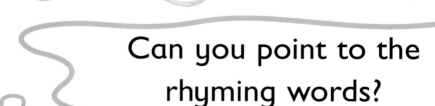

Can you point to the
rhyming words?

6